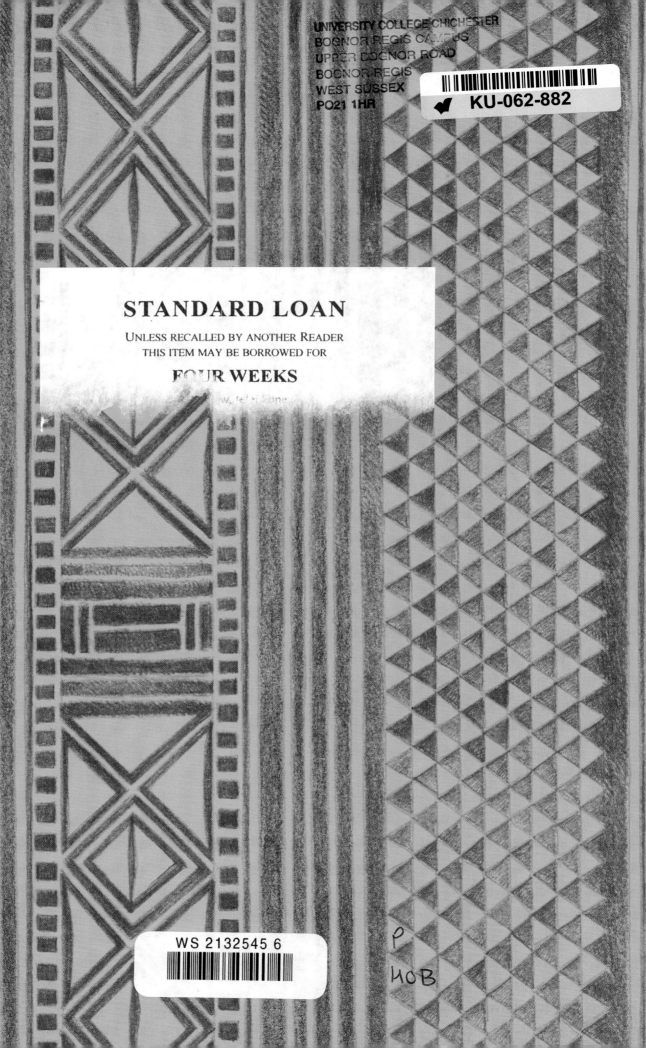

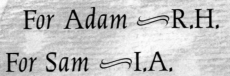

For Adam ∽R.H.
For Sam ∽I.A.
And with special thanks to Amelia, Lucy, Robert
and everyone at Walker Books

First published 2001 by Walker Books Ltd
87 Vauxhall Walk, London SE11 5HJ

10 9 8 7 6 5 4 3 2 1

Text © 2001 Russell Hoban
Illustrations © 2001 Ian Andrew

This book has been typeset in OPTICather

Printed in Italy

British Library Cataloguing in Publication Data:
a catalogue record for this book is
available from the British Library

ISBN 0-7445-7506-0

JIM'S LION

WRITTEN BY
RUSSELL HOBAN

ILLUSTRATED BY
IAN ANDREW

WALKER BOOKS
AND SUBSIDIARIES
LONDON · BOSTON · SYDNEY

From his hospital bed Jim was watching the snow whirling out of the grey sky. He was looking sad. Nurse Bami brought him hot chocolate. She was from Africa; she had tribal scars on her cheeks. She had seen lions, elephants, crocodiles.

"What's the matter?" said Bami.

"You know," said Jim.

"Tell me," said Bami. "Say it out."

"People who have what I have, mostly they die, don't they?" said Jim.

"Maybe the doctors can fix you up," said Bami.

"I've seen what they do on TV," said Jim. "They put you on a table and they put you to sleep and then they do the rest of it."

"Does that scare you?" said Bami.

"Yes," said Jim. "When I'm asleep I go to different places in my dreams but I always find my way back. I'm afraid that if the doctors put me to sleep they might send me somewhere that I can't get back from."

"Well, of course someone has to come looking for you," said Bami.

"Who can do that?" said Jim.

"Drink your hot chocolate," said Bami, "and I'll tell you."

"When you think of something, you see it in your head, don't you?" said Bami.

"Sure I do," said Jim.

"Listen carefully now," said Bami. "This is not kid stuff."

"Good," said Jim.

"You've got all kinds of things in your head," said Bami, "everything you've ever seen or thought about, all in your head."

"I can't remember it all," said Jim.

"But it's all there," said Bami, "and there are all kinds of animals in there along with everything else."

"I guess there are," said Jim.

"One of those animals is the finder who can bring you back from wherever the doctors send you," said Bami.

"Which one?" said Jim.

"That's not for me to say," said Bami. "You must find your finder by yourself."

"How can I do that?" said Jim.

"That's what I'm going to tell you," said Bami.

"Close your eyes," said Bami, "and let everything go away so your mind is empty."

Jim did that.

"Now," said Bami, "let a place come into your mind, a place where you really felt good. Don't tell me what it is, just let it come to you."

The place that came to Jim was a lonely place by the sea. It was near an empty harbour that used to be full of fishing boats. He'd been there with Mum and Dad a long time ago, before his illness.

"When you see that place," said Bami, "let yourself hear it and smell it and taste it and touch it."

Jim did that. He saw the sea and the long, long sky in the summer afternoon. There was a great brown rock that stuck out of the sea, it was called the Lion's Head. Jim saw shags flying low over the water, he heard the wind and the crying of the gulls. He heard the sighing of the sea and the hissing of it on the sand. He heard the pebbles clicking in the tide-wash.

Jim smelled the salt wind and the sea and the sun-warm rocks on the beach. He put his hand in the water, felt the deep coldness of it and tasted the salt on his hand. He touched the rocks and felt the long years in them. He felt good in that place by the sea.

"Are you feeling good?" said Bami.
Jim didn't answer. He was smiling and he was asleep.
He was in that good place by the sea. He could feel
that he was waiting for the moon to rise.
When it came up he saw that it was a full moon.
The wet sand was all silvery with it. "Here I am," said Jim,
"waiting." Then he saw a small dark shape far down the beach.
Slowly it got bigger as it moved towards him. It was a lion.

"There aren't any
lions around here," said Jim.
He ran to the cliffs on the shore
and climbed to the top
and woke up.

"Good morning," said Bami.
"Don't tell me your dream, keep it
inside you. Here comes breakfast."

"Why can't I tell you my dream?" said Jim.

"If it happened in your good place it might
be a finding dream," said Bami, "and if you talk
about it something goes out of it."

"Have you got a finder?" said Jim.

"Oh yes," said Bami, "I'd have been dead three
or four times already if my finder hadn't come
looking for me."

"Is your finder an animal?" said Jim.

"Yes, but I won't say which one," said Bami.

"How did you find it?" said Jim.

"I went to my good place in a dream," said Bami,
"and it came to me there."

"Did it, you know, scare you at all?" said Jim.

"Yes," said Bami. "That's how I knew it was the real
thing. The real thing is always more than you're ready
for. Of course I had my don't-run stone with me."

"A don't-run stone!" said Jim. "I haven't got one."

"Now you do," said Bami. She took a little
painted pebble out of her pocket and gave it to Jim.
"Don't ask me any more questions," she said.
"You must go on alone from here."

Jim's mum and dad were talking to Jim's doctor, Dr Monjo.

"Will Jim get better?" said Mum.

"It depends," said Dr Monjo, "on what Jim has going for him."

"Don't you know?" said Mum. "Haven't you done all kinds of tests?"

"Yes," said Dr Monjo, "but the tests don't always tell us why some people get better and others don't."

"Isn't there an operation you can do?" said Dad.

"There is," said Dr Monjo, "but I'm not sure he's in good enough shape for it."

"When will you know?" said Dad.

"Let's see how he is in a day or two," said Dr Monjo.

Mum and Dad brought Jim grapes and clementines and his big animal book that he'd asked for.

"Are you eating properly?" said Mum. "You have to keep your strength up."

"Yes," said Jim, "I'm eating properly and I'm feeling stronger all the time."

"That's the ticket," said Dad.

"Maybe you'll be home for Christmas," said Mum.

"I'm working on it," said Jim.

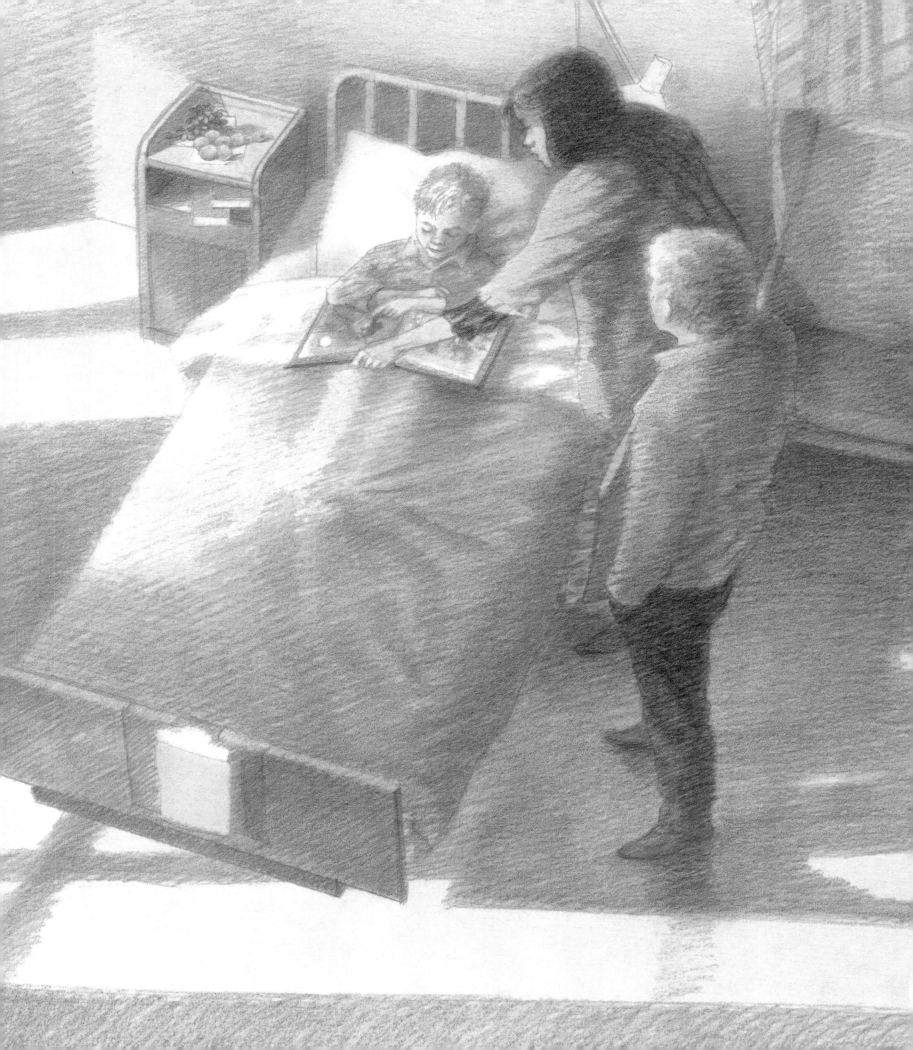

That night in his dream Jim was back at the place by the sea. The moon was still full and the lion was still coming towards him. Jim wanted to climb up the cliffs but he had the don't-run stone in his hand and he didn't. "The real thing is always more than you're ready for," he said.

Closer and closer came the lion.

"Maybe," said Jim, "everything else was a dream and this is the only thing that's real."

Closer and closer came the
lion. It opened its mouth and roared.
    "Maybe this lion will eat me up,"
said Jim, "and nobody will know
that I didn't run."
    Closer came the lion with
its amber eyes, its pink tongue
and white teeth.

    "Are you my finder?" said Jim.
    The lion roared again.
    "Maybe that means yes," said Jim.

He stood where he was until
the lion was so close that he could
smell its hot breath.

"I'm going to touch you," said Jim,
"and if you're my finder you
won't eat me up."

He stretched out his hand
as the lion came closer. Now
the lion was right in front of
Jim and he put his hand on
its head and woke up.

"Well, Jim," said Dr Monjo, "the latest tests are looking pretty good and you're looking pretty good too."

"I feel good," said Jim. He was remembering how he'd put his hand on the lion's head.

"I'll have to talk to your mum and dad," said Dr Monjo, "but first I want to talk to you. There's an operation that could help you but there's always some danger and I want you to tell me how you feel about it. Do you want to do it?"

"Yes," said Jim, "let's do it."

"You sound very confident," said Dr Monjo.

"I know you're a good doctor," said Jim, "and the rest of it I'll leave to my finder."

"Who's your finder?" said Dr Monjo.

"I mustn't say," said Jim.

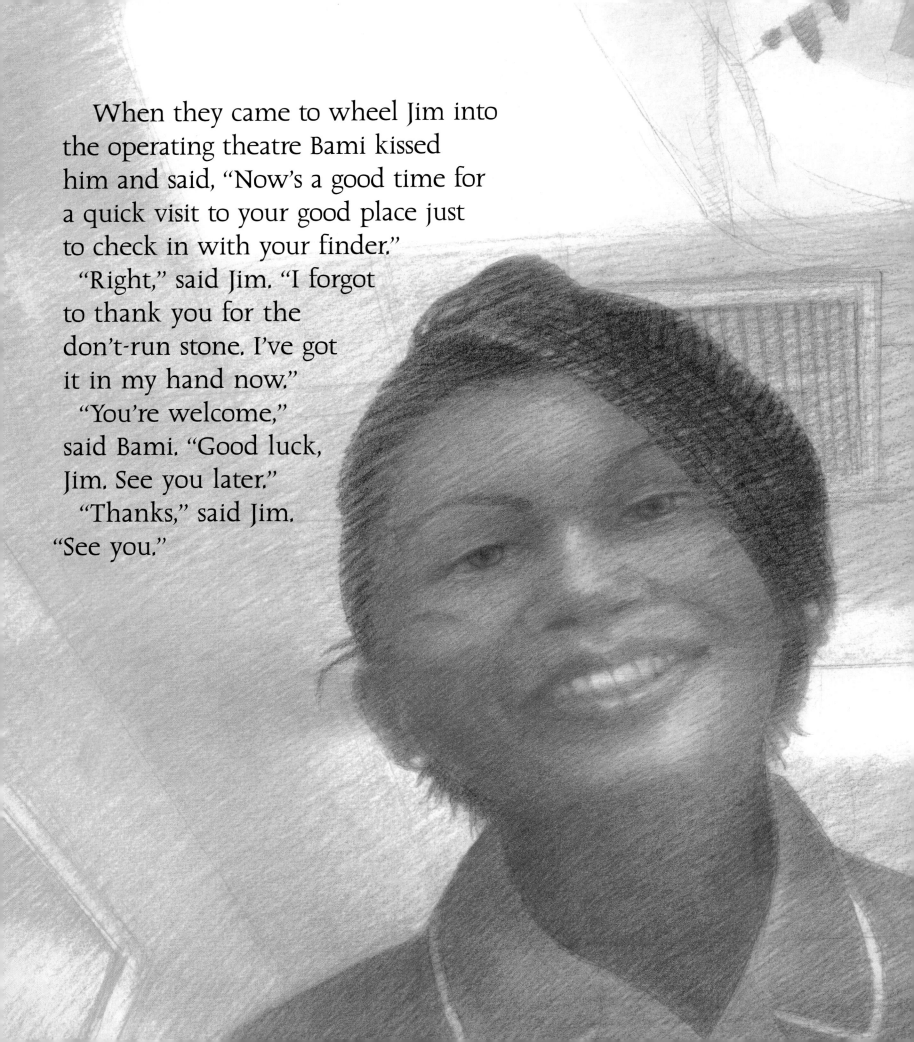

When they came to wheel Jim into
the operating theatre Bami kissed
him and said, "Now's a good time for
a quick visit to your good place just
to check in with your finder."

"Right," said Jim. "I forgot
to thank you for the
don't-run stone. I've got
it in my hand now."

"You're welcome,"
said Bami. "Good luck,
Jim. See you later."

"Thanks," said Jim.
"See you."

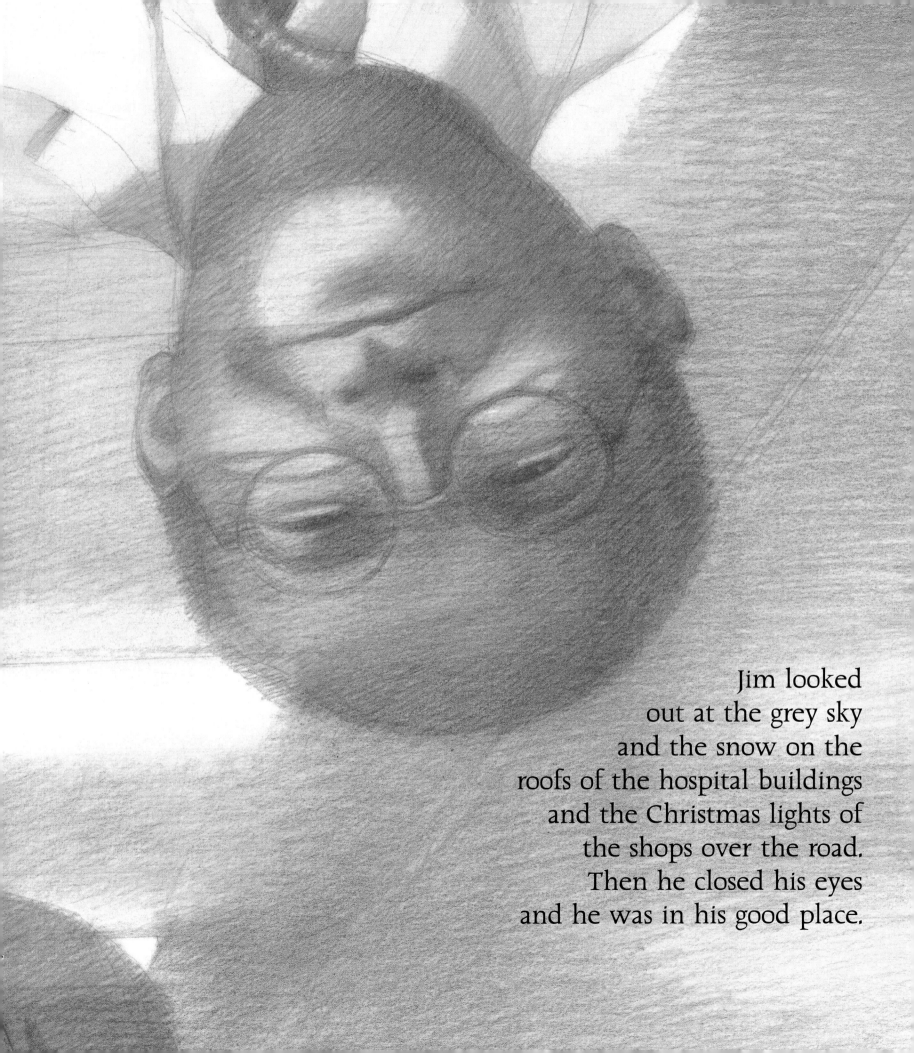

Jim looked
out at the grey sky
and the snow on the
roofs of the hospital buildings
and the Christmas lights of
the shops over the road.
Then he closed his eyes
and he was in his good place.

There was no moon but in the
starlight he could see the lion sitting
on the beach the way a dog sits.
It was waiting for him.

Jim looked into the lion's
amber eyes and the lion
opened its mouth and roared.

"OK," said Jim, "let's do it."
He walked down the long curve
of the beach into the dark
and the lion followed.

On Christmas morning Jim came downstairs in his pyjamas and looked at the Christmas tree with its fairy lights. He remembered how his lion looked coming through the dark to find him.

"Happy Christmas!" said Mum and Dad.

"Happy Christmas," said Jim. "I haven't had a chance to get your presents."

"You're our present," said Mum.

"The best that could ever be," said Dad.

Jim got a train set and a computer game from Mum and Dad. There was another box, a small one. Jim opened it and there was a beach pebble inside the wrappings.

On it was written:

This is to remember me by.
It is from my good place.

Love xx, Bami.